Fin.

THE ADVENTURES OF

ELVIS THE PUG

LOST IN CANADA

Written by:	**Daniel David Elles**
Illustrated by:	**Danica Smith** Age 9: Fourth Grade
Edited by:	**Dominic Fiordilino** Age 10: Fifth Grade
Cover by:	**Richard Eland** Uncle, Father and Grandfather.
Contributor:	**Carolyn Gianunzio** Aunt, Mother and Grandmother.

Denny
Dec 2011
D

Daniel David Elles

VOLUME I.

Copyright © 2015 Daniel David Elles.

Library of Congress Control Number: 2015917791

ISBN-10:   0996886303

ISBN-13:   978-0-9968863-0-7

Trademark: "Elvis the Pug" is currently under review for trademark by the USPTO (United States Patent and Trademark Office). Serial number: 86805613.

All rights reserved. No part of this publication may be reproduced, stored in a retrieval system, or transmitted in any form or by any means, electronic, mechanical, recording or otherwise, without the prior written permission of the author.

First Edition, November 2015.

Published by: Tiber Publishing

P.O. Box 66245

Roseville, Michigan (USA).

This book is a work of fiction. The characters, incidents, dialogues and events are fictitious. They are products of the author's imagination and not to be construed as real. Any similarity to real persons (living or dead) is coincidental and not intended by the author. The author and contributors are not responsible for, and should not be deemed to endorse or recommend, any product or website other than their own. The author and contributors, similarly, cannot be responsible for third party material.

Edited by: Dominic Fiordilino, Age Ten

ABOUT THE BOOK

This is a children's educational book – ages 7-11, along with chapters and illustrations – where an entertaining Pug puppy, Elvis, learns all about science, math, geography, animals, FAMILY VALUES, etc. Full of twists and surprises, this 90-page story will certainly capture your interest; while learniing valuable information and cherished life lessons.

Elvis, a beautiful brown Pug, was recently adopted by a loving family in the small town of St. Clair, Michigan.

One night, after a summer of fun and games, the happy Pug laid down to rest during a terrible storm. However, instead of a good sleep, he is swept away by the rugged St. Clair River and finds himself over 30 miles away from home, in Canada.

Elvis, who nearly drowned, has no idea how to get back home. The poor little Pug befriends several animals and, together, they try to help Elvis arrive home safely.

Can Elvis get all the way back to
St. Clair before dinner?

Will he become a victim of the treacherous
waters?

Daniel David Elles

ı

Edited by: Dominic Fiordilino, Age Ten

PLEASE LEARN WITH ME!

Hello, boys and girls! I am Elvis the Pug. I'm just a little puppy who wants to help my friends learn some really awesome things that will certainly make your parents proud.

Although I'm only one year old, I'm actually about the same age as you. That's right! A dog year, for me, is your age multiplied by seven. So, if I'm one year old, then you would be seven years old. And, if I'm two years old, then that makes you fourteen.

Anyway, this is a story about when I first came to my new family, in St. Clair, and I was just eight months old (around five years in your age). I got lost and ended up in Canada.

Even though I was terrified, I learned a lot of very interesting things. For example, not only did I learn about geography and science, but I also learned math, metrics and more!

So, please read about my adventure and learn with me. If you're uncertain about a word or want to find out more cool stuff, then just go to the Appendix and Glossary located in the back of this book.

Also, if you really want to learn more, then just have your mom or dad sign up on my website at: www.iamelvisthepug.com.

When you become one of my fans, you can find out so many awesome things and play some great learning games. Plus, I'll send you a personally autographed photo!

If your parents allow, you can also follow me on facebook @iamelvisthepug or even on twitter @iamelvisthepug.

Thanks for taking your time to read about my adventure. I assure you that there will be much more to come.

Your pal and friend,

Elvis

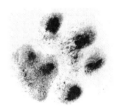

I am Elvis the Pug.
www.IamElvisthePug.com

Edited by: Dominic Fiordilino, Age Ten

DEDICATION

==

Dedicated to all the teachers, animal lovers and young readers who – through love; not hate – will make our world a better place to live.

Use whatever gifts you may have to help others. Remember that we are all more similar than we are different!

==

FYI: 10% of net book profits will go to Macomb County Care House (www.mccarehouse.org): a non-profit 501C(3) providing hope and healing to child victims of abuse for over 17 years. Executive Director: Dorie Vazquez-Nolan

September, 2015.

In the small town of St. Clair, Michigan, there lived a very fine family, in a huge house, along the beautiful St. Clair River.

Three months ago, Mr. and Mrs. Jones moved to the enchanting town, in Michigan's Blue Water Area, with their ten year old twins: Dominic and Danica.

Dominic, a strong and stocky boy, loved to play soccer and read; while Danica, a delightful and charming girl, enjoyed drawing and painting pictures of animals.

The twins truly loved their new home's huge bedrooms filled with all sorts of awesome toys and lifelike stuffed animals. Also, all of the neighborhood kids enjoyed hanging out with Dominic and Danica.

When they weren't inside their big bedrooms playing games, they would go outside and play in their gigantic backyard. And, if they weren't on the swings or trampoline, they would play tag and hide-and-go-seek.

Illustrated by: Danica Smith, Age Nine

Mrs. Jones would often observe the children playing from the home's big bay windows and occasionally yell out from the patio, "KIDS! Don't go too close to the river. It can get very dangerous. BE CAREFUL!"

All summer long, everyone had so much fun. Yet, although everything was near perfect, something just wasn't quite right.

Dominic and Danica were happy that Crazy, their orange-striped cat, came along with their move to St. Clair. However, in some sort of weird way, something was somehow missing. But no one could put a finger on it.

Edited by: Dominic Fiordilino, Age Ten

PART ONE.

ELVIS THE PUG.

Illustrated by: Danica Smith, Age Nine

Daniel David Elles

Edited by: Dominic Fiordilino, Age Ten

CHAPTER 1.

One unforgettable day, Mr. Jones – St. Clair's new Chief of Police – came home early to prepare one of his famous barbecues on the patio grill.

"Who wants burgers?" Mr. Jones asked.

"We do! We do!" Danica and Dominic happily replied, in unison.

"Can our friends stay over and eat with us?" Dominic eagerly asked.

"Absolutely! Make sure it's okay with their parents," the smiling father, taking off his police hat, answered.

"It's okay, Mr. Jones," Antonio and Gavin replied. "Danica said you would be doing a barbecue and we already cleared it with our parents, sir."

"Is that so?"

"Yeah, Dad." Danica ran to her father, smiled, and said, "I overheard Mom on the phone so. . .I told everyone about your amazing barbecues. We're all in!"

Illustrated by: Danica Smith, Age Nine

"Alright then, kids." Mr. Jones smiled and continued, "I have a question. Does everyone want one of my famous burgers or would you rather have a hot dog?"

"Come on, Dad. You know the answer," Dominic replied. "Burgers!"

"Dominic likes his burgers, but I do like hot dogs, too," Danica said.

"Well then, I guess you'll like this hot dog." Mr. Jones said, while taking out a brown Pug puppy from under his police jacket.

Edited by: Dominic Fiordilino, Age Ten

"Dad!" Danica yelled. "He's so handsome and so proud looking. . .he looks like a king. What's his name?"

"He doesn't have one yet," Mr. Jones paused. "So, why don't you name him?"

"He's such an innocent looking puppy, but he certainly does look like a king," Dominic interjected. "Let's name him. . .*KING.*"

Danica, with the happy puppy enthusiastically licking her face, replied, "I agree, but let's name him. . .*ELVIS*!"

Mrs. Jones smiled and said, "I think Elvis is a wonderful name."

"Elvis it is," Mr. Jones agreed. "Just like Elvis Presley, *The King of Rock & Roll*!"

Illustrated by: Danica Smith, Age Nine

CHAPTER 2.

Now, nothing was missing at the Jones' house. Not only were Dominic and Danica ecstatic to have Elvis, but Crazy the Cat also enjoyed the new addition to their family. And they all played together for the rest of the day.

"Okay kids. It's been a long day. Say good-bye to your friends and let's get you two ready for bed," Mrs. Jones said.

"Dad, can Elvis sleep with me? Please, Dad," Danica asked, as the brown Pug happily wagged his curly tail.

"You need to ask your mother, sweetheart."

"Mom, can he please. . .pleeease?" Danica begged. "Look how happy he is. Elvis loves me so much! See how he keeps licking me?"

"Okay, Danica. I can see that he loves you, but what about Crazy?"

"It's alright, Mom. Crazy always ends up in my bed, anyway," Dominic chuckled.

Edited by: Dominic Fiordilino, Age Ten

And so it was. For the rest of the summer, Elvis played with the kids all day; while at night, he slept with the charming Danica.

Every morning Elvis would wake up and start licking Danica's face. He was only eight months old, and puppies always had to go potty when they woke up. But Danica didn't mind. She would take Elvis to the backyard and let him run around so he could relieve himself outdoors.

"Be careful!" Mrs. Jones, cooking breakfast, would yell out. "Don't let Elvis get too close to the river, sweetheart. It's too dangerous!"

"I know, Mom," Danica would answer. "It's okay. He doesn't even like the water."

Afterwards, Elvis would race up the long backyard and jump up on the patio to eagerly eat his morning meal; which was followed by a nap, some digging, and more playing.

Everywhere Danica and Dominic went, their pleasant Pug would happily follow along. If they ate, he ate. If they played, he played. But Elvis somehow always managed to get several more snacks, along with more naps, during the day.

Illustrated by: Danica Smith, Age Nine

CHAPTER 3.

Everyone at the Jones' house was now content, and Elvis couldn't believe how lucky he was to find such a wonderful home. Everything was now picture perfect, and it stayed that way until the last day of summer.

For the past week, St. Clair's weather had changed from hot and humid to misty rain and occasional downpours. With another miserable day of rain sprinkling down, Danica decided to play indoors with her lifelike stuffed animals. From birds and farm animals to a squirrel and even a honey bee, she must have had a dozen of these realistic-looking creatures in her room.

Although it was only a soft drizzle, it was still too uncomfortable to play outside. So, scratching her puppy's ears, she asked, "Elvis, it's the last day of summer. What do you want to do, boy?"

Elvis, watching Danica play with the stuffed animals, wiggled his wing tipped ears and thought:

Edited by: Dominic Fiordilino, Age Ten

Well, I'm going to do the same thing I do today that I do every "doggone" day. I wake up, stretch, hit the backyard, eat breakfast, play, lick everyone, nap, have a snack, dig around, bark a bit, play some more, lick everyone some more, eat lunch, nap again. . .For me, this will be just another great day with my awesome new family!

"KIDS!" Mrs. Jones shouted. "There's going to be a big storm tonight. So, I want you to make sure your toys are put back in the shed."

"Okay, Mom," Dominic and Danica replied.

"That's good. Then, I need you both to get a bath and get your clothes ready for the first day of school tomorrow."

"Awe, Mom, I had a bath yesterday," Dominic moaned. "Can I just take a shower? I promise to wash really well."

"Alright then. . .but I know that Danica needs a bath. She's a complete mess from painting all of those animal pictures."

"Okay, Mom. Can Elvis have a bath, too?"

"No, sweetie. I'm going to put him on the patio and let the rain wash him." She smiled and paused, "I think the rain will make him clean."

Illustrated by: Danica Smith, Age Nine

"MOM!" Danica yelled. "Elvis is afraid of the rain. You can't do that to him!"

"I know. I know. I'm just joking, dear. But he can't sleep with you tonight. You need to wake up early."

"Okay, Mom. I understand. He can sleep alongside Crazy tonight." Danica smiled and continued, "I'll go and get his doggie bed ready."

Edited by: Dominic Fiordilino, Age Ten

CHAPTER 4.

With school starting tomorrow, Danica had to wake up earlier than Elvis. So, he had to sleep in his doggie bed near the patio and next to Crazy's cat couch.

Somehow, Elvis knew that Danica needed to sleep alone, but he hated being in the doggie bed all by himself. He wasn't accustomed to that and the rain made the situation even worse.

To comfort the sad puppy, Mrs. Jones gave Elvis a huge bone before she went to bed. But that didn't matter much. He was simply too scared to think about the bone.

As the rain was coming down hard and loudly rattling the patio doors, Elvis was still scared. And it was really raining "cats and dogs".

Crazy, about six years old, had experienced many summer storms; however, this puppy was too young, and he didn't like it very much. Looking over at Crazy soundly sleeping through the storm, he started to shake. He was the only

Illustrated by: Danica Smith, Age Nine

one in the entire house still awake. He was afraid. Really afraid.

He decided to sneak over to Danica's room and jump into her bed, but the door was shut. He then tried Dominic's room, but that didn't work either. His door was also closed and no amount of nudging could open it.

The poor puppy desperately thought, *I don't know what to do. Everyone's asleep and I'm so scared. I know they love me, but I don't think they know how afraid I am. What can I do? What can I do?*

Shaking like a scared child, Elvis had only one thing to do. He climbed into his doggie bed and tried to sleep alongside Crazy. He prayed that the storm would soon stop and hoped that the morning sunshine would soon awaken him.

With the windy and swirling rain loudly slamming against the patio doors, Elvis promptly

Edited by: Dominic Fiordilino, Age Ten

decided to engage his vivid imagination and thought:

I know it's so terribly wicked outside, with the rain so brutally coming down. But, if I could somehow just pretend to be asleep in Danica's comforting arms, with all of those cuddly stuffed animals surrounding me, I would truly be safe and everything would be okay.

And, that is exactly what Elvis did.

Illustrated by: Danica Smith, Age Nine

CHAPTER 5.

However, it was not to be. Instead of soundly sleeping with Danica and her stuffed animals, the scared puppy suddenly found himself outside in the terrible storm.

He jumped and jumped on the patio door to wake up Crazy. But it didn't work. Crazy was inside peacefully sleeping, while he was outside getting completely drenched. That's when the storm turned for the worse and large hail, the size of golf balls, began to pound him hard. Really hard.

Elvis thought, *I can't believe I'm outside. I need to find somewhere safe, or this hail is going to kill me.*

So, he quickly headed for the shed located at the end of the long backyard. If he could somehow manage to get inside the shed, Elvis knew that he would finally be safe. And, with big bolts of lightning striking across the dark, dreary sky and thunder banging louder than a marching

Edited by: Dominic Fiordilino, Age Ten

band; the poor Pug frantically sprinted for the safety of the shed.

Elvis thought, *I can wait out the storm in the shed. Then, in the morning, I'll get back inside to be with my loving family.*

Elvis knew he needed to get some rest, or this night would certainly get worse. And, just when he started to doze off; an enormous bolt of lightning hit the shed.

"WACK! BOOM! BANG!"

The steel shed was hit so hard that it was knocked off the ground, lifted into the air, and slammed into the treacherous St. Clair River.

Illustrated by: Danica Smith, Age Nine

With Elvis inside and the severe storm making the river even more violent, the shed bobbed up and down the rugged river's waves; while poor Pug banged against its walls. Before, he was only fearful of the rain; but now, as he bounced between the walls of the crumbling shed, he became frightened for his life.

The last thing he remembered was yelling for help, "Danica! Danica! Dominic! Dominic! SAVE ME! SAAAVE ME. . .PLEASE HELP ME. . .HELLLP MEEE! PLEEEASEEE!"

Edited by: Dominic Fiordilino, Age Ten

PART TWO.

I'M IN CANADA...?

Illustrated by: Danica Smith, Age Nine

Daniel David Elles

Edited by: Dominic Fiordilino, Age Ten

CHAPTER 6.

"Are you okay? Hey little puppy. . . are you okay?" Gordon the Goose asked, shaking the Pug's seemingly lifeless body. "Wake up little guy! WAKE UP!"

"Uh? What? Elvis asked, rubbing his bloodshot eyes with his tiny paws. "Who are you? What are you?"

"My name is Gordon and I'm a Canada goose," the brown-feathered bird answered, while pompously sticking out his pure white-feathered belly.

"Hi, Gordon. . .my name is Elvis."

"Well, Elvis. . .you really had me worried there for a moment," Gordon replied. "I thought you would need mouth-to-mouth resuscitation."

"I don't know what that is, Gordon."

"It's when you breathe air into somebody's lungs to help them revive. You almost drowned!"

Elvis got up, shook his waterlogged body, and said, "I know what drowning means, but are you saying that I almost didn't survive?"

Illustrated by: Danica Smith, Age Nine

"I sure am!" Gordon exclaimed. "And, by the way, I have a beak so. . .I don't think mouth-to-mouth would have worked," he laughed.

"Thanks, Gordon, but I think I may be lost," the frightened Pug frowned; and then coughed up some of the river water he had swallowed. "Where am I?"

"You're in Canada, little guy."

"What's Canada?"

"Canada is a country, Elvis," the gorgeous goose, feverishly flapping his brown wings, laughed.

Edited by: Dominic Fiordilino, Age Ten

"I've never been to Canada," the confused Pug replied. He then continued, "I've never been anywhere. I'm just a puppy, and my new family, in St. Clair, just adopted me."

"Oh, I see," Gordon said. "The St. Clair River separates Canada and the USA. Somehow, you came across the river and ended up here. That would be Sarnia, Canada."

"Oh!" Elvis exclaimed. "I need to get back home. Danica and Dominic will miss me. Can you help me, Gordon?"

"I can help you a bit, little fella. I'm a Canada goose, and my passport is only good for winter. So, I can only take you to the border."

"Border? Am I far away from home?"

"Yes, Elvis. You must be at least 50 kilometers from St. Clair."

"What's a kilometer, Gordon?"

"A kilometer is a unit of length in the metric system. It is how most countries measure a long distance," he paused. "It's similar to how Americans measure distance in miles."

"I heard about that. Americans measure in yards, but most countries actually measure in meters," Elvis commented. "Is that right?"

"Correct, Elvis. You're a pretty smart Pug," Gordon paused. "A meter is about 10% longer than a yard. And a kilometer is 1,000 meters."

"I get that, Gordon. But how far is 50 kilometers. . .in miles?" Elvis asked.

"We can certainly calculate that to miles," Gordon answered. "Since 100 kilometers is the same as 62 miles, that means that 50 kilometers is half of that so. . .that would be 31 miles."

"31 miles!" Elvis shrieked. "That sounds so far. Can I get home tonight. . .before dinner?"

"I'm afraid not, little guy. Actually, you won't get back home for several days or a week.'"

"Several days? A week? Oh my Gosh! That is such a long time," Elvis started to cry. "I already miss my family so much. I really need to get home soon, or they will forget about me."

Edited by: Dominic Fiordilino, Age Ten

CHAPTER 7.

"Hey there, Gordon, my old friend !" Sammy the Squirrel stated. "And. . .why is that handsome Pug puppy crying?"

"Hi, Sammy," the good-looking goose smiled. "This is Elvis and he's lost."

 "I see. So, that's why he's crying," he paused. "Do you think there's anything I can do to help out?"

"Can you help, Sammy? Can you please help me?" Elvis begged. "Gordon is so very nice, but he says it could take several days for me to get back to St. Clair."

"St. Clair!" Sammy exclaimed. "You sure are lost little guy. That could take a week?"

Illustrated by: Danica Smith, Age Nine

"No! No!" Elvis cried out. "That's such a long time. My new family will forget about me, and I love them so much. I miss them all so much!"

"Don't cry," Sammy, wiping the Pug's tears with his long fluffy tail, softly said.

"Hey, guys! I have an idea," Gordon interjected. "There just may be a way to get you home faster, little puppy."

"Really! You really can!" Elvis exclaimed.

"Sammy gathers nuts all summer long to store in his favorite tree where there's an owl. So, just maybe. . ."

"No!" Sammy interrupted. "We can't disturb Oscar. He hates to meet newcomers and, as you know, he's sleeping."

"Who's Oscar?" Elvis asked.

"That's funny," Gordon replied. "Oscar is a wise old owl, and he always says *Who? Who?*"

"That's not funny for me," Sammy said, crossing his squirrely eyes. "Owls don't like to be bothered. . .especially by strangers. And that would be you two."

"But you know Oscar," Gordon replied.

Edited by: Dominic Fiordilino, Age Ten

"I do. We both share the same tree."

"Well, with his wisdom, he may know a way to get Elvis home in time for dinner."

"Please, Sammy. Pretty pleeease," Elvis pleaded, with his puppy-dog eyes widely open.

"Oh. . .Oh nuts. . .okay," Sammy smiled and said. "I can't refuse those big brown eyes."

"That settles it. We're off to see the wonderfully wise Oscar," Gordon smiled.

"Like I told you, he sleeps during the day and hunts at night," Sammy briefly paused. "So, we better get going guys. And, like I always say, there's no time like the present."

Illustrated by: Danica Smith, Age Nine

CHAPTER 8.

With Sammy leading the way, Elvis and Gordon happily followed. Although it wasn't a very long journey, it was certainly scenic.

Sarnia is a very peaceful and pleasant place located where the St. Clair River meets Lake Huron, one of the five Great Lakes. (NOTE: The other Great Lakes are: Erie, Michigan, Ontario and Superior). It has a rather large countryside overlooking the blue water, with bright green grass and large trees scattered between huge farm houses.

"Wow! Canada is really beautiful," Elvis commented, trotting between his new friends.

"Thank you, Elvis. That's why I love being a Canada goose," Gordon's beak grinned.

"And why I, too, love to call Canada home," Sammy stopped and smiled.

As the trio made their way north, they approached a big white farm house, with a beautiful red barn, and decided to stop for a

Edited by: Dominic Fiordilino, Age Ten

short break. Just then, Elvis – admiring the lovely view – was so suddenly stunned that all of his brown fur bristled.

"Why are you guys staring at my house?" Horace the Horse neighed.

"You don't want any trouble now...do you?" Brian the Bull, with a nasty look, snorted and Carla the Cow angrily mooed.

"Come on guys," Sadie the Sheep baaed. "They seem harmless so. . . let's see what they want."

Illustrated by: Danica Smith, Age Nine

"Yeah! Let them speak," Chandler the Chicken softly clucked, with her head bobbing.

"Hi everyone, I'm Elvis and we're lost. I mean, I'm lost," Elvis said. "And these are my new friends, Gordon and Sammy. They're helping me get back home."

"Well, you sure are a proud-looking Pug," Sadie smiled. "How did you get lost?"

"He has no idea. I found him alongside the riverbank this morning," Gordon replied. "He's from St. Clair and. . ."

"St. Clair!" Horace neighed. "That's in America and about 50 kilometers away. My Uncle Henry lives there."

"I know! I know! Elvis exclaimed. "That's 31 miles for Americans, right?"

"Yeah. That's no bull," Brian the Bull laughed with a snort and his wife, Carla, again mooed.

Edited by: Dominic Fiordilino, Age Ten

"I'm a simple squirrel," Sammy said. "My buddy, Gordon the Goose, convinced me to help out this poor puppy. So, hey. . ."

"Don't say *HEY* or Horace will get hungry," Sadie the Sheep smiled and the others laughed.

"I was just admiring your beautiful country," Elvis paused. Then, he continued to explain, "I'm sorry, but that's the reason why we were staring at your nice house."

"Okay then, you seem to be safe and Elvis looks like a sincere little Pug. Just maybe we can help you," Chandler cackled.

"Really, you can! Really!" Elvis excitingly yelled out, while joyfully jumping and continuously licking all of the farm animals.

"Stop jumping and licking everyone," Horace instructed Elvis. "Look what you're doing to Sadie, little fella."

Caught up in the moment, Sadie was frantically jumping and lavishly licking everyone, too. The obviously happy sheep said, "I'm sorry guys, but I'm a sheep and we just follow along. You know how it is?"

"Yeah, we know how it is. Sheep certainly do follow along," Horace neighed.

Illustrated by: Danica Smith, Age Nine

With everyone loudly laughing and Chandler cackling non-stop, Carla smiled and mooed, "I think Brian can help you."

"Honey, why do you always volunteer me?" Brian continued, "I could help, but why are you going this way? St. Clair is across the river."

"We're going to see Oscar the Owl," Sammy answered, swirling his tail.

"I understand," Brian said. "But he doesn't like strangers. And that's why the wise old guy always says *Who? Who?*"

"HEY! Oops...sorry about that Horace, I didn't mean to say *HEY*," Gordon's beak grinned. "Anyway, that was my joke – *Who? Who?*"

Sammy smiled and explained, "Oscar and I share the same tree. So, we're close friends."

"That's good," Horace neighed. "We're the last farm house before you hit Sarnia city limits." He paused, "I think Brian can escort you there."

Edited by: Dominic Fiordilino, Age Ten

"I sure can. All of the neighbors know me, so they won't trouble you at all," Brian firmly snorted, confirming his support.

"Yeah, the neighbors sure like you and so do all of their cows," Carla sarcastically mooed and smirked.

"Honey, you're the only cow for me," Brian softly snorted and kissed her cheek.

"Enough you two," Chandler cackled. "We need to help Elvis out!"

"This is really great! Thank you!" Elvis exclaimed. "Thank you all so very much!"

"Elvis, can you stop slobbering over everyone? We need to go," Gordon interrupted.

"No time like the present," Sammy said.

"Okay! But I want to express my gratitude," Elvis said. "Thanks! Thank you everyone!"

Henry the Horse neighed.

Sadie the Sheep baaed.

Chandler the Chicken cackled.

Carla the Cow mooed.

And Brian the Bull escorted them towards the fence to meet Oscar the Owl.

Illustrated by: Danica Smith, Age Nine

CHAPTER 9.

Crossing the countryside farmland to the edge of the barbed-wired fence, Brian the Bull bade farewell to the trio; and Elvis expressed his appreciation with several more lavish licks.

"We're almost there," Sammy smiled and said.

"Great!" Elvis exclaimed. "I can't believe that I can make it home so soon. This is really great, guys!"

"Sammy?"

"Yes, Gordon."

"We've known each other for what. . . about five years or so?"

"Yes, Gordon."

Edited by: Dominic Fiordilino, Age Ten

"Well, why do you go this far to plant your nuts for your winter hibernation?"

"What's hibernation?" Elvis asked.

"Hibernation is when animals sleep all winter long," Gordon replied. "Right, Sammy?"

"Although I'm black, I'm actually called an Eastern Gray Squirrel. And, contrary to popular belief, we don't hibernate," Sammy replied. "We just don't like the cold. So, we don't come out much during the winter. And we just sleep a lot."

"I thought you gathered food so you could sleep all winter long," Gordon asked.

"No, my friend. We gather enough food, every summer and fall, to last us three years."

"What do you do with all that food?" the curious Elvis asked.

"We bury it near our den, called a drey, where we go for the winter," Sammy answered. "And, since our dreys are located in trees, many humans often call us *tree squirrels*."

"So, that's how you know Oscar the Owl," Elvis commented.

"Yep. We squirrels stay in our drey, with our family, all winter to stay warm. And, in case of really long winters, we gather three years of food. . .mostly nuts."

"Now, I understand," Gordon said. "Your family's drey is in the same tree as Oscar, but you gather your food near my home."

"Correct, but it's definitely nothing like your winter home," Sammy laughed.

"What do you mean by *winter home*?" the interested Elvis asked.

"Canada geese also don't like the cold. So, they fly down south to a warmer climate," Sammy answered.

"Really, Gordon?" asked Elvis. "You don't live in Canada all the time?"

"Sammy's right. We don't like cold weather."

"But I thought you liked Canada?"

"We do," Gordon replied. "We're among the last to leave the cold winter and among the first to arrive in the spring."

"Where do you go?"

"Well, when the ground begins to freeze, we migrate down south. In fact, some of my cousins go all the way to Mexico."

Edited by: Dominic Fiordilino, Age Ten

"Are you kidding?" Sammy interjected. "Geese go all the way to Mexico?"

"Where's Mexico, Gordon?"

"Mexico, like Canada, is one of America's borders. Canada is a country to the north and Mexico is a country to the south. . ."

"Together, these countries comprise the North American continent," Sammy interrupted.

"And there are only seven continents in the entire world. There's also: Africa, Antarctica, Asia, Australia, Europe and South America," Gordon explained.

"That's so cool," Elvis said. "So, even though we live in different countries, we live on the same continent, right?"

"You sure are a smart puppy," Sammy said. "And, although we're all very different, we're actually all very similar."

"Really, Sammy? How's that?" Elvis asked.

"For example, Canada geese also store food for their long winter trip called a migration."

"That's right!" Gordon exclaimed. "But, instead of storing food near a drey, we store the food in our bodies."

Illustrated by: Danica Smith, Age Nine

"What's a migration, and why do you need so much food. I don't understand?" Elvis asked.

"Migration is where animals perform a seasonal movement from one region to another region," Sammy explained. "So, since geese and other birds don't like the cold, they fly south for the winter. . .because it's warmer in the south."

"Yep! Humans and animals need energy to walk, run, fly, etc.," Gordon paused. "So, when you eat food, the body turns it to energy to help you perform your daily tasks."

"I sort of get it," Elvis said. "Can you please explain more? I really find it fascinating."

"Certainly, just as a human's car needs gas, called fuel, in order to drive; our body needs food, also fuel, in order to live."

"I see," the enlightened Elvis said. "So food is the fuel for the body, right?"

"Correct! I knew this little puppy was smart," Sammy said. "The body stores food and converts it to glucose, the fuel we need to live."

Gordon's beak beamed, "I need to eat 10-12 hours every day during the summer to store enough energy for winter migration. In fact, we can fly up to 600 miles in one day!"

"And I thought 30 miles was far!" Elvis said.

"And, like me, he spends his winter with his family," Sammy said. "Geese fly together, in a V-shaped flock formation, to the warmer climate.

"That's incredible!" Elvis exclaimed, with his brown puppy eyes wide-open. "You all have a loving family, too. . .just like me!"

"That's right," Gordon paused. "But do you know the most important thing you need to learn, little fella?"

"What's that?"

"Although we're all different, we all have much more in common," Gordon said.

"I know, like winter and family, right?"

"That's true, but much more than that," Sammy smiled. "We may speak differently and do things differently; however, we are all God's creatures. That means whether we're American, Canadian, Mexican or whatever. . .we're all very special in our own way."

Gordon's brown feathers brushed a tear from his eye as he replied, "I couldn't have said it better, Sammy."

Illustrated by: Danica Smith, Age Nine

CHAPTER 10.

The educated Elvis was now growing up. His two new buddies were helping him develop from a naïve puppy to a more aware creature from God. However, he now missed his own family even more. That's why he desperately wanted to get back home before dinner.

"Here we are guys," Sammy said. "This is my family's tree."

"All trees look the same to me, Sammy. How do you know it's your tree?" Elvis asked.

"There are over 750 different types of trees on the North American continent, little guy."

"That's a lot of trees, Sammy. Why are trees so important and what do they do for us?"

"Oh, my gosh!" Gordon interrupted. "Trees are vital for every animal and human to live on earth. But, I'll let Sammy take this one?"

"Thanks," Sammy replied. "Let me tell you about my friend Jesse Fraga. . .he loves trees."

"Please tell me more," Elvis requested.

Edited by: Dominic Fiordilino, Age Ten

"Well, Jesse isn't a squirrel. . . he's actually a very kind human, who loves the environment, and plants many trees to help squirrels, animals and; in fact, everyone on earth."

"How's that?" the inquisitive Elvis asked.

"I'm glad you asked," Sammy smiled. "Jesse always tells a beautiful story about a tree and a boy he calls "The Giving Tree". Sammy paused and continued, "Jesse knows that trees absorb carbon dioxide, which is bad to breathe, and produce oxygen. Did you know that a single tree can absorb as much as 22 kilograms of carbon dioxide in one year and convert that to oxygen?"

""I know. I know," Elvis interrupted. "If one kilogram equals 2.2 pounds, then that would be about 50 pounds in America. Am I right?"

"Elvis, you're getting even smarter," Sammy said. "And that same tree could produce over 2,700 kilograms or about 6,000 pounds of oxygen, in a year. That's called photosynthesis."

"I get it!" Elvis exclaimed. "Photosynthesis is when trees and plants convert carbon dioxide to oxygen to help us all breathe cleaner air?"

"I told you that he was one smart puppy," Gordon said, ruffling his feathers.

Illustrated by: Danica Smith, Age Nine

"I see that," Sammy replied. "But, did you know that a tree's oxygen output can support the oxygen requirements for two humans for an entire year?"

"No, Sammy. I had no clue," Gordon said.

"Well, the tree that Oscar and I use is called an *Oak Tree*," Sammy replied. "They support hundreds of different species, including 284 species of insect and 324 taxa (species, sub-species, and varieties) of lichens living directly on the tree. These, in turn, provide food for birds and small mammals. The acorns of oak trees are food for dozens of species, including jays, pigeons, pheasants, ducks, and for us squirrels."

"What's an acorn, Gordon?" Elvis asked000.

Gordon answered, "I eat grass and plant materials like: roots, leaves, stems and sprouts. But I think an acorn is a nut, right?"

"You're kind of right." Sammy said. "Since acorns have seeds, they're technically a fruit. However, because of its hard shell, they're classified as a nut."

"And you're a bit crazy so. . .that's why squirrels like nuts," Gordon loudly laughed.

Edited by: Dominic Fiordilino, Age Ten

"Don't laugh so loud, Gordon," the softly spoken squirrel said. "Not all owls are nocturnal, but Oscar is definitely nocturnal."

"What's nocturnal?" Elvis quietly asked.

"That means they sleep during the day, but they're awake and active at night" Gordon answered. "So. . .Oscar is nocturnal."

"Who? Who? Who goes there?" Oscar the Owl, nervously waking up, asked.

"Hi, Oscar. It's Sammy."

"I can see that," Oscar paused. "Who else is there with you."

"Well, my old friend, I'm with two of my friends; and we're in need of your wisdom to help us. . ."

"Hold on," Gordon immediately interrupted. Stroking his beak, he continued, "I thought that owls were blind. How can you see all of us?"

"Owls aren't blind. That's been a myth, spread by the unwise, for many decades."

Illustrated by: Danica Smith, Age Nine

"What's a decade?" asked Elvis.

"A decade is 10 years, a century is 100 years and a millennium is 1,000," Gordon answered.

"He's right," Sammy said. "And, although owls hunt at night, they're not blind. They're just one of nature's best night vision hunters."

"Is that so?" Gordon said.

"Yes, it's so. My huge eyes can see in 3 dimensions and I even have 3 eyelids," Oscar replied. "I know Sammy, but I don't know you and that little Pug puppy on your right."

"Hi, Oscar. My name is Elvis and I'm lost. Sammy and Gordon are helping me get back home for dinner, sir."

"Sir, you say?" Oscar satisfyingly smiled. "You are a very polite Pug, and it's very smart to respect your wise elders."

"Thank you, sir." Elvis answered.

"Wait a minute," Sammy interjected. "If you can't roll or move your eyes and only see straight ahead, how can you see Elvis?"

Edited by: Dominic Fiordilino, Age Ten

"Because, I can turn my head 270 degrees and even almost upside down," Oscar said, demonstrating the unusually awkward move.

"Wow! That's pretty cool, sir," Elvis exclaimed. "Even I know that's almost a complete circle. . .or, 360 degrees!"

"How can I help you, smart puppy?"

"I'm from St. Clair," Elvis paused. "Somehow I ended up in Canada this morning. Now, I just want to get home so my family won't forget me."

"Elvis, you're so handsome. You have a lovely flat face and big round eyes. . .just like me," Oscar, flapping his feathers, smiled. "I'm certain your family won't forget about you."

"Thank you, sir. Thank you very much. But I've already been gone most of the day, and I miss my family so much," Elvis, with a large tear dripping down his right eye, softly said.

"Don't cry. I can help you get home, little fella." Oscar pleasantly grinned and continued, "I'm certainly a wise old owl and that's why your friends brought you here. I definitely can help you out, but please don't cry."

Illustrated by: Danica Smith, Age Nine

Elvis leaped to his feet and danced in excitement, "Really! Even before dinner, sir?"

"Yes, before dinner. Now, stop dancing."

"How can you help Elvis?" Sammy asked.

"You need to go and see my friend, Pelican Pete, at the Blue Water Bridge. Tell him I sent you. He can take you home."

"But I thought pelicans only lived by the ocean?" Gordon asked.

"Well, most pelicans live by the seashore; however, it's true that some live in our fresh waters." Oscar answered. "It's rare, but it so happens that Pelican Pete lives nearby and he's your dream that's about to come true."

"Really! Really!" Elvis exclaimed. "He can help me. . .that's great! Thank you! Thank you so very much, sir!"

"Now, there's no need to thank me. So, just go. I need to sleep," Oscar said, as he closed all three of his eyelids.

Edited by: Dominic Fiordilino, Age Ten

PART THREE.

AMERICA...!

Illustrated by: Danica Smith, Age Nine

Daniel David Elles

Edited by: Dominic Fiordilino, Age Ten

CHAPTER 11.

As the trio quietly crept from the huge oak tree so Oscar could go back to sleep, Elvis stopped, scratched his right ear with his hind foot and asked, "The Blue Water Bridge? What's that guys?"

Sammy answered, "Gordon, I'm a simple squirrel. You're the global traveler. So. . . how about you take this one?"

"Okay. The Blue Water Bridge connects America with Canada across the St. Clair River. Its dual spans are over one mile long, and it has so much traffic that it's the second busiest crossing between the two countries."

"Wow! That's pretty cool. I really can't wait to see it," Elvis excitingly replied. "How do we get there, guys?"

Turning, Gordon crossed his eyebrows above his beak in a strange expression and said, "Sammy, do you want to take that one?"

"Me? I've been following you," Sammy said.

"What are you saying, Sammy?"

Illustrated by: Danica Smith, Age Nine

"I thought you knew where we were going."

"Hey! It's not like the wise old owl put us on some yellow brick road," Gordon replied, as he ruffled his feathers and snarled.

"Guys, we're not lost are we?" asked Elvis. "I don't think I can handle that. Not right now."

"Don't worry," Gordon consoled his new friend. He then turned towards his old friend and shouted, "Sammy! What's that buzzing sound?"

"Sounds like a bee..."

"You're right," Brenda the Honey Bee interrupted. "And it looks like you're lost!"

"We're not really lost," Sammy said. "We're only just analyzing the present situation at hand."

"Okay then," Brenda buzzed. "I'll just be on my way. See ya' and good luck."

Edited by: Dominic Fiordilino, Age Ten

"Hold on, hold on" Gordon said. "Could you point us towards the Blue Water Bridge?"

"Why certainly. But that's pretty far from here," Brenda buzzed.

"How far?" Sammy asked.

"About 10 Kilometers or so. . ."

"I know! I know!" Elvis interrupted. "If 100 kilometers is the same as 62 miles, then 10 kilometers is 10 percent of that distance. So, it would be 6.2 miles, right?"

"Wow! You're not only a majestic-looking Pug, but you're also pretty smart," Brenda replied, gracefully hovering around.

"Thank you, Brenda. My name is Elvis and this is Gordon and Sammy."

"What are you doing here?" Brenda asked.

"I'm from St. Clair and my friends are helping me get back home," Elvis said.

"Yep. My friend Oscar the Owl told us that Pelican Pete could help us," Sammy said, with his head revolving to follow the bee.

"He sure can! I know Pelican Pete pretty well," Brenda paused, now flying in slow motion. "That's why you're headed to the big bridge?"

Illustrated by: Danica Smith, Age Nine

"Yep. How do you know Pelican Pete?" Sammy asked, sitting up in a squirrel pose.

"I get the best nectar and pollen from the flowers by the Blue Water Bridge. Besides, we honey bees can fly up to 6 miles for our food!"

"What's pollen?" Elvis asked.

"Pollen comes from the male germ cells from flowers and plants," Brenda answered. "It's our food! We collect pollen and bring it back to our home called a hive."

"Like your nuts! Right, Sammy?'

"Yes, Elvis," Sammy smiled. "Brenda is a worker bee and they forage 30 kilograms of pollen for their hive every year."

"Wow! That sounds like a lot, but what is a kilogram?" Elvis asked.

"Just like kilometer measures distance in the metric system, a kilogram measures weight." Gordon answered. He then continued to explain to Elvis, "A kilogram, also called a kilo, is equal to 1,000 grams. And grams are how things are measured by most countries."

"But. . .I'm American," Elvis stated.

Edited by: Dominic Fiordilino, Age Ten

"In America, Elvis, weight is measured in pounds. And one Kilogram is equal to 2.2 pounds," Gordon said.

"So, that's 66 pounds of pollen every year," Sammy said. "For such a small insect, you either must make a lot of trips or you must have a lot of bees."

"It's both," Brenda replied. "Since we can only carry one-half of our body weight, we make 25 round-trips each time we forage pollen. And there are over 60,000 worker bees in my hive."

"And honey bees account for 80% of the pollination," Gordon said. "So, without the pollen, there wouldn't be as many fruits and vegetables to eat. That's why I love bees!"

"I get that, but do all honey bees sting?" Sammy sarcastically asked.

"No, silly. Just the worker bee stings and, when we do, we die. So, we rarely sting unless we feel threatened or our hive is attacked."

"Who attacks your hive?" Elvis asked.

"Anyone who likes the taste of honey that we make from the nectar we gather."

"Nectar? What's that?" Elvis asked.

Illustrated by: Danica Smith, Age Nine

"Nectar is a sugary substance that flowers produce," Brenda answered. "We also gather nectar to make honey in our hive."

"So, you would die to protect your family and your home? That's so brave," Elvis said.

"Thanks," Brenda replied. But honey bees don't live long. We have one Queen Bee and she lives 3-5 years. Then, there are less than 3,000 males, called drones. They don't have stingers, but when they mate with the Queen, they die."

"Really, that's so sad," Elvis softly said, rubbing his eyes with his right paw.

"Thanks, little guy. All worker bees, like me, are females. And we literally work ourselves to death," Brenda sighed. "During the summer months, we only live 6 weeks."

"Yeah, but you love your family. And so do I. Can you help me get back home, Brenda? Please. Pleeasseee," Elvis pleaded.

"Who can refuse those puppy eyes? Okay everyone...follow me!' Brenda excitingly buzzed.

"No time like the present," Sammy said.

Edited by: Dominic Fiordilino, Age Ten

CHAPTER 12.

As Brenda led the foursome to the Blue Water Bridge; Elvis, realizing he would soon be home, excitingly pranced along.

"Are we there yet? Are we there yet?"

"Almost, Elvis. Almost," Brenda buzzed.

"You see that big steel thing up ahead?" Gordon asked.

"No, I can't. I'm just a small puppy and you guys are flying up in the air."

"Yeah, Gordon. He's not that much taller than me," Sammy's soft chuckle suddenly turned into an extremely loud laugh. In fact, he was laughing so hard that he fell off the curb, and a speeding car didn't even see the little squirrel.

"S-C-R-E-E-C-H!" the swerving car's brakes belched out in a deafening roar.

Illustrated by: Danica Smith, Age Nine

"BAH-BOOM! THUMP!"

"Oh no! What happened?" Gordon yelled.

"That car almost hit Sammy and ran into the curb," Brenda frantically buzzed.

"Are you okay, Sammy?" Elvis asked.

"Yeah. . .I'm alright, guys."

"You know better than to get too close to the road!" Gordon scolded the scared squirrel.

"I do! I do!" Sammy exclaimed. "I always look both ways before I cross the street."

"Just be careful and never play too close to the road. It's very dangerous!" Gordon said.

"He's right!" Brenda buzzed. "But, now that we're all safe, I'm pleased to say we're here."

"Really! Really!"

"We are." Brenda continued, "Elvis, let me introduce you to my good friend, Pete."

Edited by: Dominic Fiordilino, Age Ten

"Hi, Elvis. I'm Peter the Pelican, but you can call me Pete," the pleasant pelican squawked. "Why did Brenda bring you to see me?"

"I'm from St. Clair," Elvis paused. "Somehow. . .I came across the St. Clair River, during the storm, and ended up in Canada."

"Well, I'm actually called an American White Pelican and I fly all around these parts." Pete continued, "I can certainly say that St. Clair is far away, little puppy."

"I know. Gordon the Goose saved me, and Sammy the Squirrel introduced me to Oscar the Owl and. . .and. . ."

"And I know," Pelican Pete interrupted. "Oscar and I go way back. He must have told you that I can help get you home."

"He did! Can you? Can you really?"

"Well, Oscar is certainly a wise old owl," Pete replied. "I sure can and I sure will."

"What's your plan?" Sammy asked. "We can't cross the bridge. . .it's too big and way too dangerous for Elvis."

"I can take him in my bill."

"What's a bill?" Elvis asked.

Illustrated by: Danica Smith, Age Nine

"It's like your mouth," Pete answered, with his long, white feathers pointing to his orange colored bill. "Although it's flat on top, I have a huge throat pouch that can carry up to 10 kilos."

"I know! I know!" Elvis exclaimed, dancing on his hind legs. "Since one kilo is 2.2 pounds, 10 kilos is 22 pounds. Am I right, guys?"

"You sure are a smart puppy," Pete replied.

"He sure is!" Gordon and Sammy said.

"That's also about 3 gallons of water," Pelican Pete added. "Unlike brown pelicans that dive for food, I swim for my food. So, when I gulp fish, I swallow lots of water."

"I understand," Brenda buzzed. "That's why your bill is so big."

"Yep. We eat four pounds of fish every day and, at 4-to-6 feet in length, we're also one of the longest bird's native to North America."

"I get it," Sammy interjected. "Since our little puppy weighs less than 20 lbs., Oscar knew you could carry Elvis in your bill. . .all the way back to America."

"Really, Pete! Really!" Elvis exclaimed.

Edited by: Dominic Fiordilino, Age Ten

"That's right. It should be no problem at all," Pelican Pete demonstrated by opening his humongous foot-long bill.

"Let's get this show on the road," Brenda buzzed.

"No time like the present," Sammy said.

"Thank you. Thank you all so very much," the elated Elvis said. "Can you guys come too? I'm so sure that Danica and Dominic will love you both."

"Sorry, but I can't make this trip. My passport south is only good during the winter," Gordon answered.

"Yeah. And I need to get home to my loving family," Sammy said.

"Okay, I understand." Elvis said. "But I have one last question. Is that okay?"

"No worries," Sammy and Gordon replied.

Illustrated by: Danica Smith, Age Nine

"What's a passport?"

"I'll take that one, Gordon smiled. "A passport is an official travel document used to travel between countries. I need it to travel south for the winter." He continued, "Elvis, don't worry, you won't need one for this trip."

Edited by: Dominic Fiordilino, Age Ten

CHAPTER 13.

After saying his farewells to his new friends and shedding several long tears, the educated Elvis jumped inside Pelican Pete's bill for his trip back home.

"How are you doing, little fella?"

"I'm okay, Pete. Are we almost there?"

"Yep. We're almost back on American soil. Just hang in there a little bit longer."

"I will! I certainly will!" Elvis exclaimed.

"Wooo! Oh, no! Hold on! We've got some bad turbulence," Pete replied.

"What's turbulence?"

"Do you feel that shaking?"

"Yeah, Pete. It's really strong."

"Well, that's turbulence," Pete paused. "It's the unsteady movement of air due to bad wind conditions. This is called *clear air turbulence* and it's the worst kind."

"What do we do," Elvis nervously asked.

Illustrated by: Danica Smith, Age Nine

"We make an immediate landing. . .NOW!"

The duo made a rather rough landing onto the green grass on the opposite side of the Blue Water Bridge.

"Where are we?" Elvis asked.

"We're in Port Huron."

"Port Huron? Where's that?"

"Like Sarnia, it's a very beautiful and pleasant city in America."

"America! Yippee!" Elvis exclaimed. "So, does that mean I'm home?"

"Almost, little fella," Pete said, examining his wind damaged feathers.

"How far am I from St. Clair? Can I make it home before dinner? Can I? Can I?"

"It's not too far. Maybe 12 miles or so..."

"Can you take me there?" Elvis interrupted. "I really miss my family so much and I don't want them to forget about me, Pete."

"Elvis, you're so smart and so cute. I really don't think anybody would ever forget about you. In fact, I will never forget about you!"

Edited by: Dominic Fiordilino, Age Ten

"Thank you. Thank you very much. But I've been gone all day, and I need to get home soon. I really do. Can you take me?"

"Elvis, my wings were damaged from the turbulence," he paused. "So, I'm sorry. I really can't go any farther."

"Oh, no! No!" Elvis cried out. "I really do appreciate all of your help. But how can I get back to St. Clair?"

"It's not far. . .just down the river, Elvis."

Just then, an ornery orange-striped cat appeared and yelled out in an angry voice, "Elvis! I've been looking all over for you! Where have you been?"

"Crazy! Oh, my Gosh! Crazy!" Elvis excitingly yelled, wagging his tail faster than a spinning washing machine. "I can't believe you're here!"

"I'm sorry to yell at you," Crazy the Cat meowed. "But Danica and Dominic have been crying all day. So, our Mom and Dad sent me out to look for you. And I ended up all the way in Port Huron."

"Really! They did? They sent you all the way here to look for me?"

"Yep. We all love you so very much and got really worried about you." Crazy briefly paused and asked, "Who's your friend?"

"This is Peter the Pelican, but you can call him Pete."

"Hi, Pete. . .I'm Crazy."

"Hi, Crazy. Your poor Pug ended up in Canada so. . .I brought him back to America. We hit some bad wind and just landed here."

"It's called turbulence, Crazy. I was in Sarnia. . .that's in Canada. I met Sammy and Gordon, who helped me to find Oscar the Owl. . . Then, Brenda the Honey Bee brought us to Pete. And then. . .and then. . ."

Edited by: Dominic Fiordilino, Age Ten

"Hold on, Elvis. Hold on! And stop jumping up and down. You can tell me about your new friends on the way home."

"Home? Really? Do you know how to get back home, Crazy?"

"I'm a cat," Crazy smiled. "Cats can go miles away from home and get back. That's why they sent me to look for you, Elvis."

"Oh, thank you. Thank you very much!"

"Don't mention it," Crazy meowed. "Pete, thank you and I bid you farewell."

"Yeah! Thank you so much, Pete. Elvis licked the pleasant pelican and continued, "I have Crazy to take me the rest of the way home. I sure hope your wings will be okay."

Peter answered, "I'll be fine. It was my pleasure to help. Take care and Godspeed to the both of you."

Illustrated by: Danica Smith, Age Nine

CHAPTER 14.

With Elvis now proudly prancing alongside Crazy, the dynamic duo made their way along the banks of the St. Clair River for home; while Elvis told the story about his time in Canada.

"Do you think we can make it home before dinner?" Elvis asked.

"I'm 100% certain we can."

"That's so great. Thank you. And every one misses me, too?"

"That's right. . .everyone. Now, just follow me and don't get too close to the river."

"Oh, don't worry. I won't. I hate the water."

Edited by: Dominic Fiordilino, Age Ten

"Whatever you do, don't fall in the river."

"Crazy, you can count on me."

After making their way through Marysville, they were now only just a few miles from home. Everything was going great until Crazy's hunger overtook him.

"Crazy, where are you going?"

"I'm hungry, Elvis, and that fisherman, over there, has some fresh fish in the bucket. I'm absolutely certain of it."

"But we're so close to home. Can't you wait a bit longer?"

"Elvis, I've been out all day long looking for you. I'm simply starving, and I really do need to eat. . .NOW!"

"Uh. . .okay, then."

"Here's what we do," Crazy smiled. "You go up and distract the fisherman. Then, I'll get in that bucket and grab me lunch."

"How do I distract him?"

"Just pretend you're lost."

"But I'm no longer lost. You found me."

"I know that, Elvis. Just flash those pretty puppy eyes of yours at him and yelp a bit."

Illustrated by: Danica Smith, Age Nine

"Uh? Yelp. . .? Okay, I can do that."

Just then, the innocent-looking Pug approached the old fisherman, Howard Hill, who was placing a freshly caught perch in a bucket.

"Ruff. Ruff." Elvis softly yelped and Howard Hill looked over.

"Hey, little guy. . .are you lost?"

As Elvis made another subtle ruff sound and Howard came over to grab him, Crazy sped to the bucket and grabbed a fish.

Turning towards Crazy, the old man ran after the cat and yelled, "I know what you two are up to. Give me back that fish!"

"Run Crazy! Run!" Elvis yelled.

"Don't worry about me, you need to run, too. Run fast. . .faster!"

"I'm coming, Crazy! I'm coming!" the excited Elvis yelled. "Wait for me!"

The old man, unable to catch Crazy, turned back to tackle Elvis and yelled, "I'll get you. Come over here. . .you tricky little puppy!" the disturbed fisherman shouted. "I'll teach you two a lesson. I promise!"

Edited by: Dominic Fiordilino, Age Ten

As Howard reached for Elvis, the scared Pug promptly evaded his grasp. Now, happily on his way to catch up with Crazy, Elvis somehow hit a slick patch of grass and tripped on Howard's bucket of freshly caught fish.

Tumbling towards the river, Elvis frantically yelled, "C-R-A-Z-Y! S-A-V-E ME . . .H-E-L-P M-E! P-L-E-A-S-E!"

"SPLASH! GULP! SPLASH!"

"ELVIS! ELVIS!" Crazy shouted.

As the speechless fisherman watched the pretty puppy being carried downstream by the rugged river, Crazy left his lunch behind.

"OH NO! OH NO!" Crazy cried. "It's all my fault! I'm to blame for trying to take something that wasn't mine." Crazy screamed out, "I'll never cheat or steal again. I'm so sorry, Elvis."

"Help me, Crazy. . . I'm drowning!"

Crazy, realizing that bad things happen to those that cheat and steal, yelled out, "Elvis, you need to doggie paddle."

"But I can't! I. . .I can't!" Elvis, gulping for air screamed out. "The waves are too strong for me! HELP ME CRAZY! H-E-L-P ME C-R-A-Z-Y! HEELLP! PLEEEASE!"

Illustrated by: Danica Smith, Age Nine

Now, even the shocked and stunned fisherman was sorry. He did his best to help and even threw out a nearby floating device. But it didn't work. Elvis was drowning.

Edited by: Dominic Fiordilino, Age Ten

PART FOUR.

THE END FOR ELVIS?

Illustrated by: Danica Smith, Age Nine

Daniel David Elles

Edited by: Dominic Fiordilino, Age Ten

CHAPTER 15.

"WAKE UP! WAKE UP, ELVIS! WAKE UP!"

The severely shaking Pug, thinking he was in "Doggie Heaven", opened up his huge puppy eyes. He had no idea what God looked like, but he was sure that the person yelling wasn't God.

"Elvis, you had a nightmare," Danica said. "You've been really rattled for the past twenty minutes or so. . ."

Uh. . .What. . .Where am I, Elvis thought, jumping to his feet.

"Good morning, Elvis," Dominic said. "Looks like you had a terribly bad dream, little guy."

"He sure did," Mrs. Jones replied. "How about you eat some breakfast, Elvis?"

"He's not even eating," Mr. Jones said. "Looks like Elvis really had a bad nightmare."

Elvis couldn't eat. Not now. He wasn't sure if he was dead or alive. So, he ran past his breakfast bowl and headed straight for Danica's bedroom.

And there it was.

Illustrated by: Danica Smith, Age Nine

All of the animals he had met were in Danica's room. The goose, the squirrel, the horse, the bull, the cow, the sheep, the chicken, the bee, the pelican, etc. . .were all there.

But none of them were talking. The seemingly lifelike animals were just sitting around, stuffed, in her bedroom. Just like simple stuffed animals. That's when Crazy the Cat began loudly meowing.

Without using any words, he gently began to nudge the handsome Pug from behind. Now, being really confused, Elvis actually started to realize that maybe, just maybe, he wasn't in "Doggie Heaven".

Quickly, he turned around, and that's when he noticed the concerned looks on Dominic and Danica's faces.

Oh, my gosh! Elvis thought. And, without hesitation, he started dancing on his hind legs, while sloppily licking both of them.

Elvis thought, *I'm alive and the luckiest Pug in the world. . .it was all just a dream*!

Edited by: Dominic Fiordilino, Age Ten

Read more about

THE *Adventures of Elvis The Pug.*

GET YOUR **FREE** SIGNED PICTURE OF ME, ELVIS THE PUG!

Sign up at: <u>www.IamElvisThePug.com</u>

On my website, you can continue to learn with me. We can do a quiz, a crossword, or even a word search.

Illustrated by: Danica Smith, Age Nine

Daniel David Elles

Edited by: Dominic Fiordilino, Age Ten

ABOUT THE AUTHOR

Daniel David Elles ("Danny") is from St. Clair and lived overseas (mostly in Hong Kong) for fifteen years. In 2005, he moved back to Michigan with his first Pug, JuJu, who passed away in March 2015. Today, he and "Elvis the Pug" live in Sterling Heights, Michigan, where he writes fiction novels for adults and children. DANNY is the proud uncle to both Danica Smith and Dominic Fiordilino, his Godson.

LOST IN CANADA is the first volume in his new children series. There are several more in the works and they will soon be published. You can find his first adult novel, "Social Media Serial Killer", on Amazon and Barnes & Noble. Or, visit www.chiefdan126.com, where you can also read a FREE 50 page excerpt.

DANICA SMITH, the illustrator, is a nine year old girl – in the 4th Grade – at Violet Elementary School of the Lake Shore Public School District locacted in St. Clair Shores, Michigan.

DOMINC FIORDILINO, the editor, is in 5th Grade at Donaldson Elementary School, of the West Allegheny School District, outside Pittsburgh, PA.

Illustrated by: Danica Smith, Age Nine

Danny, Danica and Dominic would really appreciate your feedback. You can contact them at:

Website: www.IamElvisThePug.com

Email: Elvis@IamElvisThePug.com
Danny@IamElvisThePug.com
Danica@IamElvisThePug.com
Dominic@IamElvisthePug.com
TiberPublishing@yahoo.com

Facebook @IamElvisThePug.

Twitter   @IamElvisThePug.

However, the best way to offer feedback and suggestions is to sign-up on the website or the old-fashioned way by mailing:

TIBER PUBLISHING INC.
P.O. BOX 66245
Roseville, MI 48066

Edited by: Dominic Fiordilino, Age Ten

GLOSSARY

Accustomed: customary or usual.

Admire: to look at with pleasure or warm respect.

Appreciation: an enjoyment of the good qualities of someone or something. Or a full understanding of a situation.

Awkward: causing difficulty, or a feeling embarrassment.

Bristled: hair or fur to stand upright; especially in anger or fear.

Brutally: harsh, severe.

Century: a period of 100 years.

Classified: arranged in classes or categories.

Concerned: worried, troubled, or anxious.

Decade: a period of ten years.

Dimensions: a measurable extent of some kind, such as length, breadth, depth, or height.

Distract: divert one's attention from something worrying or unpleasant by doing something different or more pleasurable.

Disturbed: a normal pattern or function changed.

Dreary: dull, bleak, and lifeless; depressing.

Drenched: wet thoroughly; soak.

Drey: a squirrel's nest

Exclaimed: yell out suddenly, especially in surprise.

Eagerly: a rather impatient desire or interest in something.

Elated: happy.

Elegant: pleasingly graceful and stylish in appearance.

Enlightened: spiritually aware.

Enormous: very large.

Escort: accompanying another for protection or security.

Ecstatic: expressing overwhelming happiness or joyful excitement

Exclaimed: yell out suddenly, especially in surprise.

Expressions: the look on someone's face to emphasize a feeling.

Fascinating: extremely interesting.

Feverishly: moving quickly to try to get a job done.

Forage: an animal searching widely for food.

Frantically: fast, nervous actions.

Frowned: an expression of disapproval or concentration.

Glucose: a simple sugar that is an important energy source in living organisms.

Gratitude: thankful or to show appreciation for kindness.

Hibernation: a state of inactivity.

Humongous: huge; really big.

Interject: say (something) abruptly; an interruption.

Illustrated by: Danica Smith, Age Nine

Kilogram: a unit of measure in the metric system (2.205 pounds).

Kilometer: a unit of measure equal to 1,000 meters (0.62 miles)

Lavishly: generously; overdoing a lot of something.

Literally: a strong feeling, not true.

Majestic: proud. having or showing impressive beauty or dignity

Meter: a unit of measure in the metric system equal to 100 centimeters or 39.37 inches (10% bigger than one yard or three feet.

Metric: the international standard of measuring.

Migration: seasonal movement of animals from one region to another.

Millenium: a period of 1000 years.

Naïve: a lack of experience, wisdom, or judgment.

Nocturnal: active at night time

Obviously: easily understood; predictable.

Ornery: stubborn; bad temper.

Passport: a document used for international travel

Pleaded: to emotionally beg.

Pleasure: happy; satisfied.

Photosynthesis: process used by plants and tress to convert light energy, normally from the Sun, into chemical energy that can be later released to fuel the organisms' activities

Pollination: to fertilize a flower, developing seeds to make more flowers and plants.

Prancing: to walk or move around with highly spring steps.

Promptly: fast; quick.

Resuscitation: revive another from unconsciousness or apparent death.

Revolving: move in a circular motion around something or someone.

Sarcastically: to mock or say something you don't really mean.

Severely: strictly; harshly; strongly.

Sighed: a long, deep breath expressing sadness, relief, tiredness.

Swirling: a twisting motion.

Treacherous: dangerous.

Trio: a set of three people or things.

Trotting: to proceed at a pace faster than a walk, lifting each diagonal pair of legs alternately.

Turbulence: a violent or unsteady movement of air or water.

Unison: simultaneous performance of action or utterance of speech.

Violent: physical force intended to hurt, damage.

Vivid: powerful feelings or strong, clear images in the mind.

Wicked: extremely unpleasant.

Edited by: Dominic Fiordilino, Age Ten

APPENDIX

Source: Wikipedia

The seven continents are: Europe, Asia, Africa, Antarctica, Australia, North America, and South America.

The Americas, or America, also known as the Western Hemisphere, comprise the totality of territories in North America and South America. Its area is 16.43 million square miles and has a population of over 953 million.

The United States of America (USA), founded on July 4, 1776, is a country of 50 states covering a vast band of North America, with Alaska in the extreme Northwest and Hawaii extending the nation's presence into the Pacific Ocean. Its capital is Washington D.C. As of 2015, the population is 319 million.

Canada, stretching from the U.S. in the south to the Arctic Circle in the north, has a population of 35.2 million and its capital is called Ottawa. The provinces and territories of Canada combine to make the world's second largest country by area. Russia is the first.

There are ten provinces: Alberta, British Columbia, Manitoba, New Brunswick, Newfoundland, Nova Scotia, Ontario, Prince Edward Island, Quebec, and Saskatchewan. There are also three territories: Northwest Territories, Nunavut, and Yukon.

The Great Lakes – formed at the end of the last glacial period around 100,000 years ago – are a series of interconnected freshwater lakes (Erie, Huron, Michigan, Superior and Ontario) located on the Canada-US border. With 21% of the world's fresh water, they are the largest group of freshwater lakes on Earth.

St. Clair, about 40 miles north of Detroit, is a city in St. Clair County's Blue Water "Thumb" area of Michigan (NOTE: They call it the "thumb" because, on a map, Michigan looks like a hand). It's bordered by Marysville and the county-seat of Port Huron to the north; while Canada is directly across from the St. Clair River.

Illustrated by: Danica Smith, Age Nine

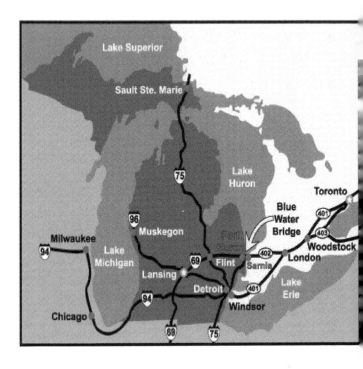

$8.99

ISBN 978-0-9968863-0-7

50899>

9 780996 886307

49796891R00051

Made in the USA
Charleston, SC
03 December 2015